The Llama Bridesmaid

With special thanks to Anne Marie Ryan.

Illustrations by Nina Jones and Artful Doodlers.

ORCHARD BOOKS

First published in Great Britain in 2019 by The Watts Publishing Group

1 3 5 7 9 10 8 6 4 2

Text copyright © Orchard Books, 2019
Illustrations copyright © Orchard Books, 2019

A CIP catalogue record for this book
is available from the British Library.

ISBN 978 1 40835 957 0

Printed and bound in Great Britain by CPI Group (UK) Ltd, Croydon, CR0 4YY
The paper and board used in this book are made from wood from responsible sources.

Orchard Books
An imprint of
Hachette Children's Group
Part of The Watts Publishing Group Limited
Carmelite House
50 Victoria Embankment
London EC4Y 0DZ

An Hachette UK Company
www.hachette.co.uk
www.hachettechildrens.co.uk

The Llama Bridesmaid

Bella Swift

Contents

Chapter One

Lulu the llama nibbled a bit of grass and looked around the field. Lambs frolicked in the pasture while their mothers grazed contentedly nearby. A gentle breeze blew, making daffodils dance and pink petals fall from the apple trees like confetti. Lulu absolutely loved springtime, when Apple Tree Farm was at its most beautiful.

The farmhouse door slammed and Lulu looked up curiously, her long, furry ears twitching. Farmer James came out of the stone farmhouse holding a toolbox, a black and white border collie at his heels. The farmer, who wore a jeans and a flat cap over his shaggy, gingery hair, wasn't old, but his face looked weary and sad. It had been a long time since Lulu had seen him smile – something he used to do every time he saw her and his wife, Rachel, together. "The Dream Team", he used to call them teasingly. Now, he barely seemed

to notice Lulu as he opened the gate and
came into the field.

"Hey, Seamus!" Lulu called out to
the sheepdog. "Where's Farmer James
going?"

"To mend the fence in the upper
pasture," said Seamus importantly.

"Maybe I can give him some help,"

offered Lulu cheerfully.

"You?" said Seamus. "I don't think so."

The farmer whistled, and the sheepdog trotted off obediently.

Lulu watched them stride across the field. She envied the sheepdog and his important job, helping Farmer James. Lulu loved to help too, but now she rarely got the chance.

Across the farmyard, chickens came strutting down the ramp leading out of their little wooden coop. The last hen to emerge was Lulu's friend Molly, followed by her four fluffy yellow chicks – Polly, Dolly, Lolly and Pip.

Lulu stuck her long neck through the

fence. "Good morning, ladies," she called out. "How are the little ones?"

"Very well," said Molly, beaming proudly at her brood as they scratched in the dirt, looking for grubs.

One chick wandered away from the others. "Come back, Pip!" said Molly, hurrying over to scold the chick.

A speckled hen with fluffy leg feathers wandered around the farmyard, peering behind an old tyre and bales of hay.

"Have you lost something, Martha?" asked Lulu. "I could help you look for it."

Martha shook her head, making the red crest on her head flap. "No, dear. I'm just looking for a good place to lay my egg."

Eventually, Martha perched on a wheelbarrow filled with hay. The chicken wiggled her bottom and fluffed up her feathers, trying to get comfortable.

Lulu turned on her hooves and headed across the field. She didn't want to distract the hens while they were laying

– she knew how important their eggs were. Farmer James sold them at the village shop.

Lulu stopped under the shade of an apple tree frothy with sweet-scented pink blossom. A heart was carved into the bark and inside it were the initials *J+R*. Lulu knew the letters stood for James and Rachel.

Farmer James's wife had been kind and gentle. She'd known all of Lulu's favourite spots to be scratched and always brought her apple slices as a treat. Best of all, sometimes she'd taken Lulu with her to work!

Rachel had worked with sick and troubled children. When Lulu came to visit, their faces would light up. Everyone loved hugging her and stroking her soft, shaggy fur. "Llamas have a calming effect on people," Rachel had liked to say. "They can make anyone smile."

Lulu blinked back tears with her long eyelashes. Even though it had been over a year since Rachel had died, she still missed her owner so much.

Rachel wouldn't want you to be sad, Lulu told herself sternly. The best way to remember her was by being friendly and helpful – just like Rachel herself.

Seeking some company, Lulu headed

across the pasture. In the upper field, the sheep were gossiping about Farmer James under Seamus's watchful gaze.

"He's in a *baaaaaad* mood again," said a sheep named Blanche. The rest of the sheep bleated in agreement.

"He's worried about the old *baaaaarn*," said her friend, Bianca. "It needs a new roof."

A fluffy lamb bounded over to her. "Mum, will you play with me?"

"I'm too tired, Albie," Bianca said, yawning. She sat down on the grass, her black legs tucked neatly under her fluffy white body.

"I'll play with you, Albie!" Lulu offered,

delighted to be able to help.

"Thanks, Lulu," said the lamb's mother.
"Run along with Lulu, Albie. She'll look
after you."

"Tag, you're it!" said Albie, butting
Lulu with his nose.

Lulu chased the lamb around the
pasture's lush, emerald-green grass.

"Gotcha!" said Lulu, giggling as she tagged the little lamb back.

"Let's play hide-and-seek now," suggested Albie. "I'll count first."

The lamb closed his eyes and began counting. "One … two … three …"

Lulu scanned the farm for somewhere to hide. In the distance she saw the ivy-covered farmhouse, and beyond it the big modern sheep shed, where she and the sheep slept at night. At the edge of the pasture stood the old stone barn that Farmer James used for storage. *Should I hide behind the old barn?* she wondered. No, that would be the first place Albie checked.

A hedge divided the pasture from the little cottage next door. Nearby was a rambling wild rose bush covered in buds. *Perfect!* Lulu thought. She trotted over to the shrub and squeezed behind it.

"Ouch!" she squealed as the prickly thorns got caught in her tan-coloured hair.

"Ready or not, here I come!" called the lamb.

Lulu kept perfectly still, not making a sound. But a moment later—

"Found you!" cried Albie.

"How?" asked Lulu.

"Your tail was sticking out!" said the lamb, laughing.

As Lulu backed out of the bush, trying to avoid the thorns, she peered over the hedge and blinked in surprise. A removal van was parked in front of the cottage.

"What are you looking at?" asked Albie.

"Someone's moving into the cottage next door," said Lulu.

Two burly men were carrying boxes and furniture from the van into the house. A short-haired lady with a camera around her neck was telling them where to put things. A girl stood next to her, fiddling with the ends of her long, dark plaits.

"I want to see too!" clamoured the

lamb, jumping up and down to try and
see over the hedge.

"Here," said Lulu. "I'll give you a
boost." She knelt down on the grass and
let Albie clamber on to her back. Lulu's
coat was so thick and fluffy she barely
felt the lamb's hooves.

"Hold tight," said Lulu. She stood up
awkwardly and—

WHOOPS! The lamb pitched forward
and toppled over the hedge into the
garden next door!

Chapter Two

"Woo hoo!" Albie bleated excitedly. "Look at me, Lulu! I'm on the other side of the hedge!"

The little lamb gambolled around the garden gleefully. The people hadn't noticed the frisky creature yet. They were too busy trying to fit a big mattress through the front door.

"Over to the left a bit," called the girl, as the lady helped hold one end of the mattress.

Lulu watched as the removal men finally squeezed the mattress into the house.

"What *is* that thing?" Albie asked, trotting back over to the hedge.

"Humans sleep on them," explained Lulu. She'd seen beds at the hospital, when she'd visited patients with Rachel.

"How silly," said Albie. "Hay is much nicer to sleep on."

The removal men came out of the house again and went back into the van.

They each came out again holding a big, brown box.

"I wonder what's in the boxes?" said Albie. "I'm going to go and find out."

"I don't think that's a very good idea—" said Lulu.

Too late! Albie had already reached the humans. *BAAAAA!* he greeted them loudly.

"Whoa!" Startled, one of the removal men tripped over Albie and dropped a box marked "fragile" on the ground.

SMASH!

"That's the crockery!" gasped the lady, her hands flying to her mouth.

The other removal man was so

surprised by the lamb streaking past that
he dropped the box he was carrying too.

CRASH!

"My toys!" cried the girl, as cuddly
toys, board games and LEGO bricks
spilled across the ground.

Albie picked up a teddy bear in his
mouth and sprinted off with it.

"Hey!" cried the girl, chasing after
Albie. "Give that back."

"You're it!" the lamb bleated, racing
away.

The girl, her mum and the removal
men all ran after Albie, but the lamb
was too quick for them. He ducked and
darted across the lawn, trampling the

flowerbeds and churning up the grass
with his little hooves.

"Gotcha!" cried one of the removal
men, grabbing for Albie's tail.

But the lamb shook him off. "Can't
catch me!" he said, laughing.

The commotion attracted the attention
of the other sheep. Soon the whole flock
gathered around the hedge, bleating
inquisitively.

"*Baaaaad* boy, Albie!" called Bianca.

WOOF! WOOF! WOOF! Seamus
bounded over. "Move it, you lot!" barked
the sheepdog sternly. "Go back to the
sheep shed."

Most of the sheep followed the

sheepdog's order immediately. A few stragglers lingered, curious to see what was going to happen, but Seamus snapped at them and they soon hurried after the others.

Farmer James ran over, his cheeks flushed. "I'm so sorry!" he called. "I have no idea how my lamb got into your garden."

"I bet I can guess," muttered Seamus, glaring at Lulu accusingly.

"I'm James," said the farmer, extending his hand over the hedge. He nodded towards the farmhouse in the distance. "I live here at Apple Tree Farm."

"I'm Meera," said the lady with the

camera around her neck, shaking his hand. She put her arm around the girl. "And this is my daughter, Avani."

The girl peeped curiously out at Lulu.

"We rented Damson Cottage because we wanted to be closer to nature," said Meera, smiling at Farmer James. "But we hadn't expected to meet animals quite so soon!"

"Is that a llama?" Avani asked shyly.

"Yes," said Farmer James. "Her name's Lulu."

"Do you keep her for her wool?" asked Meera.

"Oh, no," said Farmer James, laughing. "I keep the sheep for their wool, but not

Lulu. We got her as a guard – to protect the flock from foxes. But she's so gentle she wasn't much use as a guard. Lulu became more of a pet, and my wife trained her to be a therapy llama."

"That's fascinating," said Meera. "I hope I get to meet your wife soon."

"She passed away a year ago," said Farmer James, looking awkward.

"Oh, I'm so sorry," said Meera.

"Does Lulu bite?" asked Avani.

Farmer James smiled. "The only things she bites are apples."

Avani reached over the hedge and held out her hand to Lulu.

"Actually," said the farmer, "llamas

prefer to smell your face to get to know you."

Avani closed her eyes as Lulu leaned over the hedge to sniff her face. She giggled as Lulu exhaled, blowing warm breath on her face.

"That feels funny," said Avani, giggling.

"She likes you," said Farmer James.

"I like her too," said Avani.

"You're welcome to come and visit her any time," said Farmer James.

SNAP! SNAP! Avani's mum's camera clicked away as she took pictures of Avani patting Lulu.

"Er, I should probably take Albie home," said Farmer James, glancing over at the lamb, who had abandoned the teddy and was munching the primroses in the flowerbed.

The farmer whistled and Seamus yipped, "Albie! Get over here NOW."

"Aww," complained the lamb. "You're no fun." But he trotted over to the hedge obediently.

"Would you mind passing the little guy over to me?" said Farmer James.

Avani caught Albie under his belly and lifted the lamb up. She handed him over the hedge to the farmer as her mother snapped more pictures.

"I'll be *baaaaaaack*," bleated Albie.

"Not if you know what's good for you," barked Seamus, chasing the lamb back to the sheep shed.

"Well, nice to meet you," said Meera, putting the cover on her camera lens. "I should probably start unpacking." She headed back to the removal van and carried a box into the house.

Avani followed her mum, but turned to

give Lulu a little wave goodbye.

She's nice, Lulu thought. She hoped she'd see Avani again soon.

"Come on, Lulu," said Farmer James, ruffling the tufty hair on her head.

Lulu and the farmer walked across the pasture together. When they reached the apple tree, Farmer James stopped and sighed. "I miss her, Lulu," he said.

"Me too," said Lulu. Even though the farmer didn't understand her words, she knew he understood how she felt. She nuzzled his hand gently to comfort him, and Farmer James buried his face in her shaggy neck.

"It's so hard running the farm on my

own, Lulu," the farmer confided in her. "The bills are really mounting up. I'd hate to do it, but sometimes I wonder if I should just sell Apple Tree Farm and make a fresh start."

What? thought Lulu, hardly able to believe her fluffy ears. If Farmer James sold the farm, what would happen to all the animals who lived there? This was their home.

Lulu had to find a way to help Farmer James – and save Apple Tree Farm!

Chapter Three

COCK-A-DOODLE-DOO! Dandy
Dan, the farm's cockerel, woke the
animals up at dawn the next morning.
Lulu pawed the straw in her stall
impatiently. She couldn't wait for Farmer
James to let her out into the pasture. She
was hoping to see her new friend again!

As soon as the farmer let the animals out, Lulu raced to the hedge to see into the cottage garden. The removal van was gone, but there was no sign of Avani or her mum.

Disappointed, Lulu wandered over to see what the sheep were up to. The lambs were all crowded around Albie, eager to hear about his adventure.

"What's it like on the other side of the hedge?" asked one of the lambs.

"Awesome," boasted Albie. "The grass over there is *much* tastier than our grass. And I got star treatment – they all wanted to have their pictures taken with me!"

"Wow!" said his friends, impressed.

Seamus bounded over. "Move along," he barked at the lambs.

As the lambs ran off to join their mums, the sheepdog turned to Lulu. "You were supposed to be looking after Albie yesterday," he said accusingly.

"I just gave him a boost," Lulu protested. "I didn't mean for him to fall over."

"Farmer James is busy enough as it is," scolded Seamus. "He doesn't need you and that naughty little lamb making more work for him."

Lulu remembered how worried Farmer James had sounded yesterday. The last thing she wanted was to make things more difficult for him. *I'm going to find a way to help Farmer James*, Lulu promised herself.

All morning long she tried to think of what she could do. As she watched the hens pecking in the farmyard she suddenly had an idea.

I know! she thought. *I'll gather up the eggs.*

The hens liked to hide their eggs, laying them wherever they thought the farmer wouldn't find them. Lulu set to work, hunting for eggs in all the chickens' favourite hiding places. *I can do this!* she thought happily. It was just like playing hide-and-seek with Albie!

Aha! she thought, discovering a brown egg behind a bush.

She stuck one long leg out and prodded the egg with her foot to get it out. It rolled over. She gave it another nudge and—

CRACK!

Her nails broke the egg
open. Gooey yellow yolk
spilled on to the ground.

"Hey!" squawked
Martha. The
hen strutted over
to Lulu, her head
thrusting backwards and forwards.
"What do you think you're doing? Eggs
don't grow on trees, you know!"

"I'm so sorry," said Lulu. "I was trying
to help."

Lulu looked around, trying to think of
another job she could do. She saw a sack
of turnip seeds resting against the side

of the old barn. Farmer James planted
a crop of turnips every spring and used
them to feed the sheep in the winter.

That's it! Lulu thought. *I can help him
plant the seeds.* She'd seen the farmer
scatter the seeds in the soil before, and it
didn't seem too difficult.

Lulu bit the canvas sack with her teeth
to get at the seeds.

RIIIPPPP! Tiny purple seeds spilled
out on to the ground.

SQUAWK! "Over here, girls!" Martha
called to the other chickens. "Lulu's
found us a feast."

The hens bustled over, clucking greedily,
and began to peck at the turnip seeds.

"Thanks, Lulu," Martha said. "Sorry I was a bit cross with you – this more than makes up for the egg."

"These aren't for you ..." Lulu tried to explain.

But the chickens were too busy gobbling up the seeds to pay any attention.

WOOF! WOOF! WOOF! Seamus came running over. "Clear off," the sheepdog snarled at the hens.

Squawking and flapping their wings, the hens scattered. Lulu ran off, too, not wanting to get told off by the sheepdog again. Wandering across the field, she found Farmer James removing a tyre from his rusty red tractor.

"I really need to replace this old thing," the farmer muttered to himself.

A replacement tyre was propped against a nearby tree.

He's got his hands full, thought Lulu, *so I'll wheel the new tyre over to him.*

She stuck her head through the tyre and tried rolling it along, but it was too heavy to budge. And when Lulu tried to get her neck out of the tyre, she found that she was stuck. The air valve had got caught in her shaggy hair.

Lulu let out a strangled cry. "Help!"

"Oh, Lulu," said Farmer James, looking up from his work. "What have you done

now?" The farmer carefully untangled
Lulu's hair, releasing her from the tyre.
"Off you go," he said, giving her a pat.
He rolled the new tyre over to the tractor
and heaved it on to the wheel.

Oh dear, thought Lulu. Every time she
tried to help, she made things worse!

After a tasty lunch of tender spring greens, Lulu wandered around the pasture, racking her brain to think of jobs she could do. Her head aching, Lulu settled down under a shady tree to take a nap. *Maybe I'll dream up a way to help Farmer James,* Lulu thought as she drifted off to sleep.

Waking up later that afternoon, Lulu heard a voice call, "Hi, Lulu."

Clambering back to her feet, Lulu saw her new neighbour waving to her over the hedge.

Avani! Lulu hurried over excitedly and stuck her head over the hedge. The little girl patted her neck, then she scratched

Lulu behind her ears, just the way
Rachel had always done.

Lulu let out a gentle rumbling noise to
show Avani how much she liked it.

"I brought you something," said Avani,
holding out an apple slice. "I saved it
from my lunch box."

My favourite! thought Lulu, snaffling
up the sweet, crisp fruit.

As Avani fed Lulu apple slices, she told
her about her day.

"I had to start my new school today,"
Avani said. "It was horrible – I didn't
have anyone to play with at break time.
And a mean girl named Stella said I talk
weird."

Avani looked close to tears. Humming with concern, Lulu nuzzled the girl's face sympathetically.

Avani giggled. "That tickles."

Lulu's heart swelled with happiness as she saw that Avani's frown had been replaced by a big smile.

"See you tomorrow, Lulu," said Avani, giving her one last pat.

The next day, Lulu was waiting for Avani after school. And the next day, and the next. Avani always had a special treat for Lulu – and told her what had happened at school.

"Today Stella hid my PE kit," she told Lulu as she fed her carrot sticks. "I don't know why she hates me so much."

The following day she reported, "Stella broke my special strawberry-scented pencil. The one Dad gave me."

Lulu liked most people, but she didn't like the sound of this Stella!

"I wish my mum and dad hadn't got divorced," Avani told Lulu. "Then I wouldn't have had to move here and go to that stupid school." Tears welled in her eyes and she whispered, "I really miss my dad."

Lulu hated to see Avani so sad.

SLURP! She gave her a sloppy kiss, licking up the salty tears that trickled down the girl's cheek.

Avani rested her face against Lulu's soft fur. "Thanks, Lulu. I always feel better after talking to you."

Lulu loved her chats with Avani. So when Avani didn't appear by the hedge as usual one grey, cloudy day, she began to worry.

Where can she be? Lulu wondered anxiously.

She headed to the other side of the field, which ran alongside the country lane. Craning her neck to see down the road, she saw Avani trudging home from school. But something was very wrong: Avani's knee was bleeding, her cardigan was torn, and tears streamed down her face.

Oh no! thought Lulu in alarm. *I need to get help – fast!*

Chapter Four

Looking wildly around her, Lulu spotted Seamus across the field, watching over the flock.

"Seamus!" Lulu gasped, galloping over to him. "Get Farmer James! Avani is injured and needs help!"

The sheepdog took off barking,

streaking across the field in a blur of black and white.

A moment later, Farmer James came running out of the old barn.

"Over by the road!" Lulu called, racing back to where she'd seen Avani. *Please let her be OK,* she thought desperately.

Letting out urgent yips, Seamus led the farmer across the field. They found Avani sitting on a grassy verge, her shoulders shuddering with sobs. As if in sympathy, rain began to fall in heavy drops.

"What's wrong, Avani?" Farmer James asked, climbing over the fence.

She shook her head, too upset to speak.

"Let's get you to shelter," Farmer James

said as the rain fell harder. "The barn's closest." He picked Avani up in his strong arms, carried her over the fence and crossed the field with long strides. The rain was beating down so heavily now that Lulu could barely see as she trotted after them.

"Lulu!" whimpered Avani.

"Come inside, you two," Farmer James called, beckoning to Lulu and Seamus.

Inside the old stone barn, Farmer James sat Avani down on a hay bale and took out his phone. "Do you know your mum's number?" he asked Avani.

Wiping tears from her eyes, Avani entered the number into his phone.

"Hi, Meera," said the farmer. "This is James from next door. Avani's been in some sort of scrape. We're in the old barn."

Farmer James took a clean handkerchief from his back pocket and wiped the blood off Avani's knee. Lulu hummed with concern as Avani winced.

"Sorry. Does it hurt badly?" Farmer James asked.

"It stings a bit," Avani said, biting her lip as the farmer gently dabbed her knee.

Lulu knelt down by Avani. The little girl stroked her soft fur and gradually tears stopped spilling down her face.

"Avani!" cried Meera, bursting into the barn, soaking wet. She ran straight to her daughter and wrapped her arms around her. "What happened?"

"It was nothing, Mum," said Avani. "I, er, fell down on the way home from school." She held out her arm, showing her a rip in her sleeve. "I tore my cardigan again."

"Don't worry about that," said Meera, giving her daughter another hug.

Lulu had a feeling Avani wasn't telling her mum what had really happened. Sure enough, as Farmer James showed Meera around the barn, Avani told Lulu the truth.

"Stella tried to steal my school bag," Avani whispered in her ear. "And when I wouldn't give it to her, she pushed me over."

Stella was such a bully! It made Lulu spitting mad. *Why isn't Avani telling her mum what's going on?* she wondered.

"Stella says if I tell on her, I'll regret it," Avani said softly, as if she could read

Lulu's mind. "And I don't want to worry Mum."

Avani got up and went over to join her mother, who was gazing up at the old wooden beams.

"This barn is absolutely gorgeous!" said Meera, pushing her dripping wet hair out of her face.

Farmer James frowned. "It needs a new roof. The animals live in the new barn – I just use this for storage."

"It's got real potential," said Meera, running her hands over the thick stone walls. "It would be a perfect place to have a wedding."

Farmer James laughed, looking around

at the rusty farm equipment and muddy tools. "You must be joking," he said.

"Mum would know," said Avani. "She takes photographs at weddings."

Meera nodded. "Farms are very popular wedding venues. Your land has beautiful views – and I can just imagine this barn all decorated with white flowers."

That sounds lovely! thought Lulu.

"You could charge a lot of money," Avani piped up.

"Well ..." Farmer James said doubtfully, scratching his beard.

"Why don't I take a few photos when the weather improves?" offered Meera.

"I can put them on my website and see if you get any interest."

Lulu didn't know much about weddings, but if there was a chance it could help Apple Tree Farm, it was worth trying! *Go on,* she thought, nudging the farmer with her nose.

"Well, I guess it couldn't hurt to try ..." said Farmer James.

★ ★ ★

On Saturday morning, the sun was shining. Meera and Avani came over first thing. As Avani played with Lulu, Meera got straight to work.

CLICK! CLICK! CLICK! Meera snapped pictures of the old barn from lots of different angles.

Curious, Lulu wandered over and sniffed the camera's long lens.

"I'm sorry Lulu keeps photobombing you," said Farmer James.

"It's fine," said Meera. "Having her in the pictures just adds to the charm."

As Meera continued to take pictures, Farmer James drove his quad bike across the field. Not long after, the sheep came across the pasture like a big, fluffy cloud. Farmer James drove behind them, moving them forwards, while Seamus circled around the sides, keeping the flock together. "Move along, ladies," the sheepdog barked. "Time for your makeovers."

Farmer James stopped by Lulu. "I need your help today."

Lulu held her neck high with pride. Finally, Farmer James had a job for her!

"What's she going to do?" asked Avani.

"It's shearing day," explained Farmer James. "The sheep need a haircut."

"Lulu is going to cut their hair?" asked Avani, her eyes wide.

Farmer James chuckled. "No, she's just going to help keep them calm."

"Can we stay and watch?" asked Avani.

"Only if we won't be in the way," her mother added hastily.

"Sure," said Farmer James.

Inside the new barn, Farmer James put the sheep into a big pen. Then he took one sheep – Albie's mum, Bianca – into a separate pen with a pair of electric clippers attached to the wall. Lulu was waiting there patiently.

"*Baaaaack* off!" protested Bianca. "I don't need a haircut!"

"Don't worry," Lulu told her calmly. "Farmer James won't hurt you."

"But I like my hair the way it is!" bleated Bianca.

"Short hair is really trendy," Lulu

assured her. "And it will keep you cooler in the summer."

Eventually, Bianca stopped bleating.

"Wow," said Avani, who was hanging over the side of the pen with Meera. "Lulu managed to get the sheep to settle down."

"Other animals find llamas comforting to be around," said Farmer James.

"Avani certainly enjoys spending time with Lulu," said Meera, putting her arm around her daughter. "I think that llamas must have a soothing effect on people, too."

"Definitely," said Farmer James, nodding. "My wife used to say that

that was why Lulu made such a good therapy animal."

Holding Bianca with one arm under her front legs, Farmer James ran the clippers over the sheep's body, starting with her belly and moving around to her back. *BUZZZZZZ!* In just a few minutes, a pile of creamy white wool was heaped on the floor.

Farmer James released the sheep, who looked about half her normal size without her thick fleece.

"This is a *BAAAAAAAD* look for me," bleated Bianca. Her fleece was so short you could see the pink skin underneath.

"It will grow back," Lulu said.

Farmer James took Bianca into a separate pen, and went to fetch another sheep. One by one, he gave them each a haircut.

When all of the sheep had been shorn, Avani asked, "Are you finished now?"

"Nearly," said Farmer James. "Lulu needs a haircut too."

What?! Lulu backed away from the clippers nervously, her ears flat to her head.

"Don't worry, Lulu," said Avani. "It won't hurt."

"Could you sing to her?" asked Farmer James. "Lulu loves music. My wife used to sing to her all the time."

"I'll sing her the song we sang in assembly today," said Avani. She began to sing sweetly.

As she listened to the song, Lulu's ears relaxed and she stopped trembling.

BUZZZZZ! Farmer James ran the clippers around Lulu's middle. Her shaggy, soft fleece began to pool on the

ground. When her haircut was over, Lulu shivered. *I feel ridiculous*, she thought.

"Don't worry," Avani said, winking. "It will grow back."

Chapter Five

The following weekend, Lulu heard
Seamus barking as she grazed in the
field. Looking up, she saw Avani and her
mum coming up the gravel drive. This
time, Meera didn't have her camera, but
was holding a tablet in a flowery case.

"Hi, Lulu!" called Avani. She reached

over the fence to stroke Lulu's velvety
nose.

Farmer James was in the henhouse,
gathering eggs. When he came out of the
little wooden building, holding a basket
of eggs, Avani gasped.

"You cut your beard!" she said,
pointing at the farmer's smooth face.

Farmer James blushed. "Well, I thought
if Lulu and the sheep had a trim,
I probably should too."

"It's a big improvement," said Martha,
nodding her head and making her red
crest jiggle.

Molly, surrounded by her chicks,
clucked in agreement. "Yes, he looks

handsome without that scruffy beard."

Lulu thought Farmer James looked much better, too, but not just because he'd shaved. It was because he was smiling!

"Mum's got good news," Avani said.

"There's been some interest in the farm on my wedding website," said Meera. She held up her tablet, and Lulu saw a picture of a lady with what looked like a white sheet on her head.

Now the farmer's smile faded. "I don't know anything about organising weddings," he said. "When we got married, Rachel arranged everything."

"Don't worry. I know lots of people

who can help," said Meera. "Is now a good time to set up some appointments?"

"I've got to deliver these eggs to the village shop," said Farmer James, glancing down at his basket.

"I can take them," offered Avani. She skipped out of the farmyard, swinging the basket.

Oh, please take me with you, Lulu thought, trotting after her friend on the other side of the fence.

Avani ran back up the drive. "I think Lulu wants to come with me," she told the grown-ups.

"Do you want to take her?" asked Farmer James.

"Seriously?" said Avani, her eyes wide. "You can take a llama for a walk?"

"Not all of them," said the farmer. "But my wife trained Lulu to walk on a lead. There's a special halter in the barn, but it hasn't been used since Rachel passed away. I'm sure Lulu would love to go for a walk with you."

"Is that safe?" asked Meera, looking worried.

"Oh, yes," said Farmer James. "Llamas are very intelligent creatures. Lulu's better trained than most dogs."

"Rude," said Seamus, sniffing indignantly.

"Please, Mum," pleaded Avani.

"Well, OK," said Meera. "If you're sure it's safe."

"Yay!" cried Avani.

Farmer James disappeared into the old stone barn. When he came out again, he was dusting off a blue halter which Lulu recognised. Her ears and tail perked up. *Yippee! I'm going for a walk!*

Opening a gate, Farmer James led Avani into the field. He held out the halter to Lulu, who trotted over eagerly. Lulu lowered her neck, making it easier for the farmer to slip the halter over her nose. Then Farmer James clipped a long lead on to the collar.

"Lulu, come," he said, clicking his

fingers. The farmer started walking and Lulu trotted along next to him obediently.

"Heel," he said, holding up his hand. Lulu instantly came to a stop.

"Turn around," Farmer James said, making a circling motion with his hand. Lulu spun around on the spot.

"Wow!" said Avani. "She knows so many commands."

"Here's another one," said Farmer James. "Lulu – kiss." He touched his finger to his nose.

SLURP! Lulu licked the farmer's face.

Avani and Meera giggled as Farmer James wiped his sleeve across his face.

"Your turn," said Farmer James, handing the lead to Avani.

Avani practised walking Lulu up and down the drive, clicking her fingers whenever Lulu stopped walking.

"You're doing great," said Farmer James. "Just keep the lead nice and loose."

The basket of eggs in one hand and the lead in the other, Avani headed off again, this time with Lulu ambling along by her side. As they strolled down the country lane, Lulu stopped frequently to sniff things or nibble a new plant. It felt so good to be out and about again!

"Come on, Lulu," said Avani, laughing. "At this rate we'll never make it to the shop."

In the village centre, a group of children were kicking a football around on the green. Lulu thought the game looked fun. Her tail perked up with interest. *Maybe Avani and I can play, too!*

But then a tall blonde girl shouted at a boy wearing a football shirt. "I can't believe you missed the goal, David!" the girl yelled. "You're such a loser!"

"Oh no," muttered Avani. "It's Stella. Quick – let's go back." She waved her hand in the air, telling Lulu to turn back.

Too late! The children had already caught sight of them. Abandoning their football game, they ran across the green.

"Look!" cried David. "A llama!"

"Hi, Avani," said a girl with glasses and a friendly smile. "What's your llama called?"

"Hi, Katie," said Avani. "Her name's Lulu."

"Now I know why you smell so bad," said the blonde girl, glaring at Avani with cold grey eyes. "You live in a zoo."

"That's not very nice, Stella," Katie said quietly.

"I don't smell," said Avani, looking close to tears.

"Avani lives in a zoo! Avani smells like poo!" chanted Stella.

Lulu's ears flattened against her head. She kept her eyes on Stella, worried that the bigger girl was going to hurt Avani.

Stella reached out and snatched the basket off Avani's arm.

"Give that back!" said Avani.

"Who's going to make me?" taunted Stella. She looked inside the basket and a cruel grin spread across her face. "Oops!" she said, dropping the basket.

CRACK! Eggs fell out of the basket and smashed on the ground. Yellow goo spilled out of broken eggshells.

That was the last straw! Lulu's instincts

took over. She knew she had to protect
her friend. Puckering her lips, she took
aim and—

PTUI!

"Ew!"
shrieked
Stella.
"Your
llama spat
at me!"

All of the children burst out laughing.

"Lulu showed you!" chuckled David.

"Serves you right for being so nasty,"
said Katie.

Stella stomped off in a huff, wiping
llama spit off her face.

Good! thought Lulu. She didn't spit very often – but Stella had threatened Avani!

"Here," David said, kneeling down and putting an egg back in the basket. "Some of them are still OK."

"Thanks," said Avani.

"Can I stroke Lulu?" asked Katie.

Avani nodded. Soon, all of the children

who'd been playing football clustered around, stroking Lulu. Lulu hummed happily – she loved making new friends!

"I wish I had a pet llama," said David.

"She's not my pet," Avani said. "She lives at the farm next door to me."

"Can I come and visit her some time?" asked Katie.

"That would be cool," said Avani.

After delivering the unbroken eggs to the village shop, Avani took Lulu back to the farm. Meera and Farmer James were sitting in the sunshine, drinking tea.

"How was your walk?" asked Meera.

"Some of the eggs got broken," Avani told Farmer James. "Stella from my class threw the basket on the ground."

"What?" gasped Meera. "Why would she do something like that?"

"She's not very nice," said Avani. "She's the one who tried to steal my school bag and pushed me over."

"She sounds like a bully," said Farmer James.

"I wish you'd told me about this sooner," said Meera. "I'll speak to your teacher at school."

"Oh, I don't think Stella will be bothering me again," said Avani. "Thanks to Lulu." Then she grinned and tapped her nose.

SLURP! Lulu gave her a big kiss.

Chapter Six

As April turned into May, the weather grew warmer. Bright blue cornflowers bloomed in the pasture. Lambs frolicked in the afternoon sunshine as their mothers munched sweet clover and daisies.

Lulu waited for Avani by a hedgerow

that frothed with lacy white cow parsley, hoping her friend would be back from school soon.

"Guess what, Lulu!" cried Avani as she ran out of the cottage, wearing her gingham summer uniform and a big smile on her face. "I played freeze tag with Katie and David at playtime."

Lulu clucked her tongue to let her friend know she was delighted. Avani had been much happier since making friends, and Stella hadn't bothered her again.

"I'm glad it's the weekend, though," said Avani, stroking Lulu's nose. "Because I'll get to see more of you!"

On Saturday morning, Farmer James seemed even busier than usual. He hurried through his chores, filling up feed buckets and mucking out the sheep pens. As he topped up Lulu's water trough, he was so distracted that water sloshed over the side.

What's up with Farmer James? wondered Lulu. She tried to nuzzle him reassuringly as he let her out of her stall.

"No time for cuddles today, Lulu," said Farmer James, leading her and the sheep into the pasture. As soon as the gates were open, Seamus rounded them up.

"You've all got to be on your best behaviour today," the sheepdog barked.

"It's a big day for Farmer James."

"Don't tell me he's shearing us again," groaned Bianca. "My fleece has *baaaarely* started growing back."

"Maybe he's taking us to the agricultural fair," bleated Blanche. "I bet I'll *baaaaaag* a blue ribbon this year. Have you seen how shiny my hooves are looking?"

"Quiet!" barked Seamus impatiently. "You're not getting shorn and the agricultural fair isn't until the autumn."

"Oh no!" shrieked Albie. "I bet the vet's coming! I don't want an injection!"

The sheep starting bleating anxiously.

"Settle down!" yelped Seamus.

"Nobody's getting a jab. Some people are coming to visit Apple Tree Farm to see if they want to get married here."

Ohhhhhh! thought Lulu, suddenly realising why Farmer James had seemed so anxious.

"Yoo-hoo," called a familiar voice. Meera came down the path, followed by Avani and a girl in glasses. It was Katie, Avani's new friend. "We thought you might want some moral support this morning," said Meera.

"Thanks very much," Farmer James said. "I'm not very good at this sort of thing."

Avani and Katie went over to the

fence. Lulu stuck her neck over and sniffed Katie's face curiously.

"Is she going to spit at me?" Katie asked nervously.

"No," said Avani. "I looked it up online – llamas only spit when they're angry or feel threatened."

"That makes sense," said Katie, grinning. "Stella *is* pretty scary."

"She's not bullying me any more," said Avani, scratching behind Lulu's ears. "My mum went into the school and spoke to Mrs Logan about it. Stella apologised for all the mean stuff she's done. She's having a tough time at home – and I guess she took it out on me."

HONK! HONK! HONK! A sleek
sports car rumbled down the gravel drive,
blaring its horn and startling all the
animals. An elegantly dressed woman in
sunglasses and high heels stepped out of
the car and sniffed the air, a disdainful
look on her face. A tall man followed her.

"Welcome to Apple Tree Farm," said
Farmer James, going over to greet them.

"I'm Jasper Lloyd-Forbes," said the
man, who had a pink sweater tied
around his shoulders. "And this is my
fiancée, Petra."

"Charmed, I'm sure," said Petra. She
shook Farmer James's hand, then wiped
her hand on her skirt.

Jasper glanced at the chunky gold watch on his wrist. "We're seeing other venues today, so we don't have much time. Show us what you've got here, there's a good man."

"The barn's this way," said Farmer James, leading everyone across the field to the old stone barn. Petra clung to her fiancé's arm, her high heels sinking into the grass. Lulu trailed after them curiously.

Petra wafted her hand in front of her nose. "Can you do anything about the smell?"

Lulu sniffed the air, confused. *I don't smell anything.*

"It's the countryside, darling," said Jasper.

The lady grimaced.

Farmer James flung open the barn doors. "The barn's over three hundred years old," he told the couple proudly. "The farm's been in my family for generations."

"There's plenty of space for a live band and dancing," said Meera.

"Eeek!" screamed Petra. "A spider!"

She ran out of the barn blindly, frantically brushing a cobweb out of her hair.

BUMP! She crashed right into Lulu.

"Aaargh! What is that – that – that

BEAST?" shrieked Petra.

"That's just Lulu," said Avani. "She's harmless."

"Ugh!" Petra said, looking down in disgust. "I've got sheep poo on my new shoes!"

"Sorry, old chap," said Jasper. "I think this place is a bit too, er, rustic for us." He handed a business card to Farmer James. "Look me up if you ever want to sell this place – the land would fetch you a pretty penny."

Jasper and Petra hurried back to their car. As they sped down the drive, leaving tyre tracks in the gravel, Farmer James sighed. "Maybe this was a bad idea …"

"Don't worry," Meera said reassuringly. "That was just one couple. Plenty of other people will like it here."

"Yeah!" called Avani, as she and Katie turned cartwheels on the grass. "We LOVE it here!"

Not long afterwards, the next couple arrived. Lulu could hear them squabbling even before they got out of their car.

"We're late because *she* told me to take a wrong turning," said the man, slamming the car door.

"Only because *you* were going so fast I couldn't read the signs!" the lady shot back angrily.

"Why don't we show you around?"

said Meera smoothly. She and Farmer James ushered the bickering visitors towards the barn.

"It's not big enough," said the lady, shaking her head. "There are three hundred people on our guest list."

"I keep telling you I want a small wedding!" shouted the man.

"Well, we don't have to invite your horrible parents," snapped the lady. "That would cut it down by two!"

Soon, the couple were soon having a blazing row in the middle of the field.

"This is *baaaaaad!*" bleated Bianca. The sheep ran to the upper pasture to get away from the noise.

Although Lulu didn't like the shouting either, she stuck around in hopes that she might be able to calm the visitors down with a cuddle. But they ignored her completely.

"That's it!" shrieked the lady, yanking off her engagement ring and throwing it at the man. "The wedding's off!"

Still arguing, the couple drove away without bothering to say goodbye.

"Yikes!" said Meera. "Good riddance."

They all burst out laughing.

The last couple to visit that day seemed lovely.

"Your farm is beautiful," the bride told Farmer James warmly.

Lulu hurried over to the sheep, who
were grazing in the upper pasture.
"It's safe to come back," she told them.
"There's a new couple that really like the
farm."

The sheep, bleating with excitement,
followed Lulu across the field to check
out the couple.

Suddenly, the lady's nose turned red
and tears streamed out of her eyes.

ACHOOO! ACHOOO!
ACHOOOOOOO!

"This is a lovely place," said the
man as the sneezing woman dabbed
her streaming eyes with tissues. "But
unfortunately, Ellen has a severe wool

allergy. I'm afraid we won't be able to get married here."

After Meera took Katie and Avani home for tea, Farmer James leaned on the fence, watching the sun set beyond the distant hills. Lulu went over to him and nuzzled his hair.

Farmer James stroked her soft neck and sighed. "I'm really not sure what I'll do if nobody wants to have their wedding here, Lulu." He pulled Jasper's business card out of his pocket and stared at it. "Maybe I should take that man up on his offer and sell the farm."

No way, thought Lulu. *You can't do that!* Apple Tree Farm was Farmer

James's home – and hers. She had sworn to help Farmer James and she wasn't going to give up now!

Chapter Seven

The following Saturday, Lulu was dozing
in the pasture, enjoying the sun's warmth
on her back. Overhead, blackbirds and
skylarks sang sweetly from their nests
in the apple tree. Lulu's nose twitched,
picking up the perfume of rose petals, the
earthy smell of a freshly ploughed field

and the clean, lemony scent of the sheets flapping on the clothesline.

"Hi, Lulu!" called Avani.

Lulu's eyelashes fluttered open and she saw Avani coming down the drive with her friends Katie and David, all holding paintbrushes, trays and rollers. Meera, wearing dungarees, came behind them, carrying a bucket of white paint in each hand.

Lulu ran over to the fence, hoping that Avani and her friends would come into the field and play with her.

"We'll play with you later," promised Avani. "But first we have work to do."

"What's all this?" asked Farmer James,

walking over and setting down the bucket of chicken feed he was holding.

"We thought we'd give you a hand sprucing up the barn," said Meera.

"But you've helped me so much already …" protested Farmer James.

"Hey, what are neighbours for?" said Meera, smiling.

"Besides, you bring us yummy fresh eggs every day," said Avani.

"Let's make a start by clearing out the barn," suggested Meera. As Lulu looked on curiously, they all got to work, carrying out old farm equipment and loading things into the back of Farmer James's truck. Soon it was piled with rusty rakes and pitchforks, an old wheelbarrow with a broken handle and an ancient wooden plough.

"That thing belongs in a museum," said David, laughing.

"My great-grandfather probably used it," said Farmer James.

When the barn was empty, Farmer James wiped his forehead with the back of his hand. "Phew! That was thirsty work. Who wants a drink?"

Don't mind if I do, thought Lulu, lapping up some water from a trough.

Farmer James went into the farmhouse and came back out with orange squash and a radio. "I thought we could have some music while we work."

After they all had a drink, they made a start on the painting. The sound of a lively pop song floated out of the barn as they worked. Lulu peered into the barn, nodding her head and humming along to the music.

Inside, Meera and Farmer James were rolling paint on to the walls, turning the dull stone to dazzling white. On the other side of the barn, the children were painting with brushes, their clothes covered in drips and splatters.

"A-V-A-N-I," said Avani, spelling out her name in white paint.

That looks like fun ... thought Lulu.

The barn doors were open, so she wandered inside. The music was loud and nobody noticed her come in. There were still two walls to paint.

I'll help them, decided Lulu. Copying the way the children dipped their brushes in the paint, Lulu stuck her foot into the paint bucket.

CLONK! The bucket tipped over and paint puddled on to the floor. *Oopsie!* Lulu backed away – making a trail of white hoofprints – and bumped into the freshly painted wall. Craning her long neck, she saw a big patch of white on her tan-coloured bottom.

"Oh, Lulu!" groaned Farmer James.

"What are you doing now?"

Trying to help! But as usual, she'd made a mess of it.

"Why don't you kids give Lulu a bath?" suggested Meera. "James and I can finish off the painting."

Farmer James fetched a bucket, sponges and special shampoo from the sheep shed. Then Avani clipped Lulu's lead on to her harness and led her out into the farmyard.

The hens crowded around to see what was going on.

"Look at Lulu!" cackled Pip. "She's got paint on her bum!"

Lulu stuck her tongue out at Pip and the other chicks giggled.

"I hope Lulu likes having baths more than my dog does," said David as Avani uncoiled the hose. "Bailey hates it when we stick him in the bathtub."

"Lulu's too big to fit in the bath," said Avani, giggling. "So she's going to have a shower instead."

Avani aimed the hose nozzle at Lulu. *SQUIRT!* A blast of cold water sprayed her.

Yikes! Lulu tried to run off, but Katie kept a firm grip on the lead.

"Sorry, Lulu," said Avani, "we've got to get you clean."

The cold water wasn't so bad once Lulu had got used to it – it was actually quite refreshing.

Lulu hummed happily as Katie and

David scrubbed her back with soapy water. *This is bliss*, she thought as Avani rinsed the suds off with the hose.

"Can I have a go with the hose?" asked David.

Avani turned, and accidentally sprayed David with water.

"Hey!" David's eyes widened and for a moment Lulu thought he was going to get angry, but instead he laughed. He chucked the bucket of water at Avani and cried, "Water fight!"

SQUAWK! The hens took cover in the chicken coop as soggy sponges flew through the air like missiles. The three children ran around the farmyard,

flinging sponges and squirting each other with the hose. Even Seamus joined in the fun, barking as he cooled down in the hose's spray.

"What's going on out here?" asked Farmer James, coming out of the barn.

Just then, Avani threw a wet sponge. It hit the farmer right smack in the face. *SPLAT!*

Water dripping down his face, Farmer James

115

laughed – then tossed the sponge back Avani.

When the water fight was over, they all flopped in the grass to dry their clothes off in the sun. Tucking her legs underneath her, Lulu lay down next to Avani, resting her head in the girl's lap.

"We didn't just get Lulu clean," said Avani, tickling Lulu's chin. "We got ourselves clean too!"

The farmer and Meera sat next to each other and smiled as they watched the children stroke Lulu. Eventually Farmer James got to his feet and said, "I'll make us some lunch. I don't know about the rest of you, but I'm starving!"

Meera and the children rolled some
big wooden barrels over to use as tables,
and arranged hay bales around them
for seats. Farmer James carried out a
tray of sandwiches, crisps, strawberries
and lemonade and set it on one of the
makeshift tables. "Dig in, everyone!"

Lulu sniffed at the picnic inquisitively.

"Can I give Lulu a crisp?" asked
David.

Yes, please, thought Lulu, her mouth
watering.

"I'm afraid not," said Farmer James.
"It might upset her tummy. But you can
give her a strawberry."

As Lulu munched her strawberry,

she noticed two people wandering up the drive holding hands. They were both wearing hiking boots and carried rucksacks on their backs.

"Hello?" called the lady, fanning herself with a map.

"Sorry to bother you," said the man, "but we're a bit lost. We're looking for the White Hart pub."

"You're not far," said Meera. "Just turn right at the end of the drive and carry on to the village centre."

The couple thanked them and were about to head off when Farmer James said, "You look hot. Would you like a drink?"

The hikers, who were called Sarah and Tim, sat down on a hay bale and gratefully accepted some lemonade.

"What a beautiful old barn," said Sarah, sipping her drink.

"Thank you," said Farmer James. "We've spent the morning painting it. I'm hoping to start hosting weddings here."

Sarah and Tim exchanged a look.

"We're actually looking for a place to have our wedding," said Sarah. "That's why we're heading to the pub. But every place we've seen is booked up for months."

"Would you mind if we take a look

around the farm?" asked Tim.

As the couple admired the barn, Lulu wished she could tell them that Apple Tree Farm was the perfect place to get married. Looking around wildly, she saw the white sheets flapping on the washing line. An amazing idea suddenly popped into her head. She'd just have to *show* them!

Lulu ran to the washing line and pulled down the white sheet with her teeth. With the sheet over her head like a veil, she hurried back to the barn, hoping she looked like the bride she'd seen on Meera's tablet. But as she ran the sheet slipped over her eyes. *CRASH!* She

bumped straight into the happy couple, spilling their cups of lemonade all over them.

"Oh, Lulu!" said Farmer James, handing Sarah a handkerchief. "I'm so sorry about that!"

But Sarah was laughing. "I'm fine," she said, stroking Lulu. "I love llamas. They're my favourite animal."

"We really like this place," said Tim. "Is the barn available the first weekend in July?"

Farmer James gulped.

Sarah's face fell. "Oh no! Do you already have a booking?"

"No, it's not that," said Farmer James.

"It's just that it's only three weeks from now …"

Tim nodded. "We don't want a long engagement. We can't wait to get married – and this seems like the perfect place to have a party."

Farmer James glanced nervously at Meera and she smiled encouragingly.

Don't give up now! thought Lulu, butting the famer gently with her head.

"OK, then," the farmer said, nodding. "Let's do it!"

"Hurrah!" said Sarah, throwing her arms around her husband-to-be and giving him a kiss.

"Yay!" said Avani, clapping her hands.

Lulu's ears twitched and her tail swished with excitement. There was going to be a wedding at Apple Tree Farm!

Chapter Eight

Over the next couple of weeks,
preparations for the wedding were in
full swing. Farmer James was even busier
than usual, but he did his chores with a
smile on his face. The farmer whistled
as he planted lots of pretty purple and
yellow pansies in old water troughs

outside the old barn.

"He's in a good mood these days," bleated Bianca.

"It must be the *baaaaalmy* weather," said Blanche.

But Lulu thought the real reason was that Farmer James liked spending time with their neighbours. Meera was going to take photos at the wedding, and she'd helped organise the florist and caterer, too.

"I wouldn't have been able to do this without your help," said Farmer James, as he and Meera hung bunting outside the barn.

"I'm happy to help," said Meera.

"Keeping busy has helped take my mind off the divorce."

Farmer James smiled sympathetically. "Yes, it's hard getting used to being on your own."

"Do you still miss your wife?" asked Meera.

"I'll always miss Rachel," Farmer James said, attaching one end of the bunting to a wooden beam. "But she'd want me to be happy."

Lulu, who was listening, nodded her head. Rachel had been very kind. She'd have been glad that Farmer James and Lulu had found nice new friends.

At last, the big day arrived. Everyone

was so excited they woke up before
Dandy Dan crowed *COCK-A-
DOODLE-DOO!*

As Farmer James led the animals into
the field, the sheep gossiped about the
wedding.

"I wonder if they'll have a live
baaaaaand," said Bianca.

"Do you know where they're going
on honeymoon?" asked Blanche. "I hear
Baaaaaali is lovely."

"Everyone mind their manners today,"
Seamus barked at the sheep. "That goes
for you, too," he said, looking at Lulu.

"Bossy paws," Lulu said, sticking out
her tongue. She knew how important

today was for Farmer James – she would
do everything she could to make it
perfect!

"Can you *baaaaabysit* Albie for a bit?"
Bianca asked Lulu. "I want to see the
bride arrive."

"Of course," said Lulu.

"Let's play hide-and-seek again, Lulu,"
bleated Albie.

As Lulu played with the lamb, a steady
stream of people arrived. First came
Avani and Meera. As they blew up white
balloons and hung them around the
barn, the florist arrived in a little van. He
set down a beautiful bouquet outside the
barn and began unloading vases of pink

and white roses. Next, the baker drove up, delivering a cake with three layers decorated with icing flowers.

"Ooh, that looks delicious," said Albie.

"I didn't think sheep liked cake," said Lulu.

"I'm not talking about the cake," said the lamb, eyeing the bouquets hungrily. "Roses are my favourite – dee-lish!"

The lamb pranced over to the bouquet and began to munch the roses.

"No, Albie!" cried Lulu. "That's for the wedding!"

"I'm just having a few nibbles," said

the lamb through a mouthful of petals. "Nobody will notice."

But when the florist came out of the barn he shrieked so loud Lulu's ears hurt. "The bride's bouquet is ruined!"

"Oh no," said Farmer James, running over. "This is a disaster."

Meera looked at her watch. "We've got half an hour before the bride arrives. We need to find a replacement."

Farmer James looked around desperately. "How about these?" he suggested, pointing to the pansies in the water troughs.

"No!" said the florist. "They won't do. The bride asked for roses!"

Lulu suddenly remembered the rose bush she'd hidden behind when she'd played hide-and-seek with Albie. She nibbled the end of Avani's plait to get her friend's attention.

"Sorry, Lulu," said Avani, tugging her plait away. "I can't play right now. I need to find some roses."

But I know where they are! thought Lulu, frustrated. *How can I get them to come?*

"Seamus," she called to the sheepdog. "Can you get Farmer James to follow me? It's important!"

The sheepdog sprinted across the grass. He skidded to a halt in front of Farmer

James and began to bark urgently.

"What's the matter, boy?" asked Farmer James. "Is something wrong with the sheep?"

"This way!" cried Lulu, running across the field.

Seamus took off after her, with Farmer James chasing behind. Lulu led them to the rose bush. The sheep had nibbled the flowers at the bottom of the shrub, but the higher branches were still full of fragrant pink flowers.

"Roses!" shouted Farmer James, waving to the florist. "I've found some roses!"

The florist hurried over. "They'll do

nicely." He quickly cut some off and tied them into a bouquet.

Just then a car rumbled down the drive – the wedding guests were starting to arrive!

"I'd better put the sheep inside," said Farmer James. "I don't want to risk them causing any more trouble. You too, Lulu," he added, taking hold of her harness.

As the farmer shut her into her stall, Lulu felt left out. She stuck her long neck out of the window, watching the wedding guests arrive holding presents wrapped in shiny paper. She wanted to be out there, where all the fun was! The bridesmaids arrived next, wearing pink dresses and flowers in their hair. Finally, a fancy black car drove up and the bride stepped out, wearing a white lace dress and a long veil.

Wow! thought Lulu. Sarah looked beautiful!

The florist hurried over and handed her the bouquet he'd just made.

"It's gorgeous," said Sarah, smiling.

Phew!

The sound of music came from the barn – *DUM DUM DE DUM, DUM DUM DE DUM* – and the bride, holding her bouquet, went into the barn.

"Hi, Lulu," said Avani, leaning over the door to Lulu's stall. "Mum said I needed to stay out of the way, too, so I thought I'd keep you company." She sighed. "It's so unfair – I really wanted to see the wedding."

Me too, thought Lulu.

A crafty look suddenly crossed Avani's face. "I bet if we're really, *really* quiet, nobody will even notice if we peek in."

Avani opened Lulu's stall door and clipped the llama's lead on to her harness. She led Lulu to the old barn and they peered around the doorway. Lulu hardly recognised the barn. It was festooned with flowers, bunting and balloons. The guests, perched on hay bales decorated with silky white ribbons,

sat on either side of an aisle. A lady in a black suit stood at the front with Sarah and Tim.

"You may now kiss the bride," the lady announced.

Lifting up Sarah's veil, Tim kissed his wife.

CLICK! CLICK! CLICK! Meera snapped pictures of the newlyweds as the wedding guests cheered.

Lulu's heart swelled with happiness as music began to play. It was all so wonderful she couldn't help humming along to the song.

"Shh!" whispered Avani, holding her finger to her lips. But it was too late –

the guests were looking around to see where the sound was coming from.

"Oh my goodness!" whispered a lady in a purple feathered hat, pointing at the doorway.

"Look, Mummy!" cried a little boy in a sailor suit. "It's a llama!"

Everyone turned to stare at Lulu. But Lulu was looking at Sarah and Tim. The bride and groom clutched each other, their shoulders shaking. They were crying.

Oh no, thought Lulu. *I've spoiled their wedding.* Even worse than that, she'd let Farmer James down. The future of Apple Tree Farm depended on this wedding –

and now she'd ruined it. She hung her head in shame.

"It's OK, Lulu," whispered Avani. "Look."

Lulu lifted her head and saw tears glistening in Sarah's eyes.

"They think it's funny!" explained Avani.

The bride and groom were crying … with laughter!

"Come outside, everyone," said Sarah, chuckling. "So you can all meet Lulu."

The newlyweds walked down the aisle arm in arm, leading their guests out of the barn. As Meera took pictures of the happy couple under the apple tree –

including one with Lulu – the wedding
guests crowded around to stroke the
llama.

"She's so soft!" said a man in a suit.

"What a sweetheart!" said the lady
in the purple hat, as Lulu nuzzled her
cheek.

"Is she your pet?" the little boy in the sailor suit asked Avani, who was holding Lulu's lead carefully.

"I wish she was," said Avani. "But I just live next door."

"I'm getting married next autumn," said one of the guests. "Maybe I'll have my wedding here, too – I'm crazy about llamas."

Much later, after the guests had eaten their dinner and Sarah and Tim had cut the wedding cake, a band set up on the grass and began to play. Everyone danced along, under the glow of the stars and fairy lights strung from the apple trees. Lulu nodded her head and shuffled her feet to the beat as Avani twirled around on the grass, barefoot.

"Care to dance?" Farmer James asked Meera, holding out his hand.

"I'd love to," said Meera, smiling. She took off her camera and danced into the farmer's arms.

Just before midnight, the bride and groom left for their honeymoon. But before they left, Sarah threw her bouquet in the air. "Catch!" she cried.

"Oh!" said Meera, blushing as pink as the roses that landed in her hands.

"You know what that means," said the lady in the purple hat, winking. "You'll be the next to get married!"

One year later ...

DUM DUM DE DUM! DUM DUM DE DUM! Lulu's long ears twitched, hearing the Wedding March coming from the old barn. That was nothing new. Over the past year, Apple Tree Farm had hosted weddings most weekends – with Lulu as the star attraction. Lulu was so proud that she'd been able to help Farmer James. The wedding business was such a big success that he'd been able to buy a new tractor and replace the leaking roof on the barn. But today's

wedding was extra special, because Lulu was going to be a bridesmaid!

"Are you ready?" asked Avani, adjusting the little white veil on Lulu's head and the wreath of pink and blue flowers around her neck.

Lulu nuzzled her friend's face, humming happily.

"Careful," said Avani, giggling. "You'll mess up my hair."

Avani's long hair was twisted into a pretty crown on top of her head. She wore a swishy light-blue dress, and sparkly silver pumps on her feet. In her hands, which were covered in swirly henna designs, she held a basket of rose

petals. Avani was a bridesmaid, too.
Because today her mum was getting
married … to Farmer James!

"Let's do this, girls," said Meera, smiling
at them. The bride looked stunning
in an ivory sari with beautiful gold

embroidery. Instead of a veil, she wore a gold headpiece.

"You look beautiful, Mum," said Avani, hugging her mother.

Then, holding Lulu's lead, Avani walked down the aisle, to where Farmer

James was waiting with the officiant. The farmer looked awkward but proud in his new grey suit and he beamed when he saw them approaching.

"Awwww!" sighed the wedding guests as Lulu and Avani went past. Lulu spotted Avani's friends sitting near the front. David winked at her and Katie gave her a thumbs-up.

As the bride and groom exchanged their vows, and promised to love each other for ever, Lulu thought her heart would burst with happiness. A few weeks earlier, Meera and Avani had moved into the farmhouse. Now, Apple Tree Farm rang with laughter, music and chatter again. Farmer James wasn't lonely any more – and neither was Lulu!

As the bride and groom kissed, Avani threw her arms around Lulu's neck.

"I love you, Lulu," said Avani, tapping her nose.

SLURP! Lulu gave Avani a big sloppy kiss. Because she loved Avani right back – and she always would!

The End

Love stories about animals?
Read on for a sneak peek …

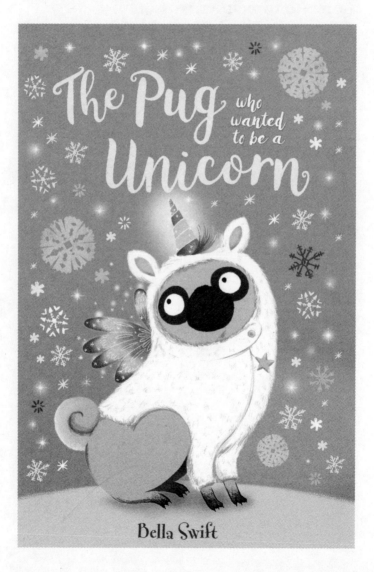

Peggy wriggled her little bottom and
snuggled closer to her two brothers and
two sisters. The five little pug puppies
were curled up against their mother's
side, snoozing in a furry heap of paws
and curly tails. Sighing dreamily, Peggy
nuzzled her squashed black nose against

her mum's soft, tan-coloured fur.

Suddenly, her mum stood up, nudging the dozing puppies awake with her nose.

"Hey!" yelped Peggy's brother Pablo. "I was sleeping."

Yawning, the puppies clambered to their feet.

"Today's a very important day for all of you," announced their mum, gazing down at the puppies fondly with big brown eyes. "You're going home."

"Aren't we already home?" asked Peggy, puzzled.

"You're twelve weeks old now," her mum said gently. "So your new owners are coming today. They are taking you

to your forever homes."

Peggy stared at her mum in confusion,
her wrinkled forehead creasing even
more. *Forever home? What's that?*

"Don't worry, little ones," the puppies'
mum reassured them. "For every dog,
there is a perfect owner. I know you
will all find yours and be happy in your

forever homes."

SLURP! SLURP! SLURP!

A rough pink tongue licked Peggy's face clean.

"Muuuuum!" protested Peggy, trying to squirm away from her mother's sloppy kisses.

"Don't wriggle," said her mother. "I want you to look your best." With one final slurp, she moved on to wash Peggy's sister Polly.

When all the puppies' fur was clean, their mum looked at them proudly.

"There! Now you're ready to meet your new owners."

"I hope my owner has a big garden," yipped Peggy's brother Paddy, panting with excitement.

"I hope my owner gives me lots of tasty treats," yapped Pippa, the greediest puppy of the litter.

"I hope my owner likes to take naps," said Pablo, yawning. He stretched out his front paws, sticking his bottom in the air.

"What about you, Peggy?" asked her mum gently. "What type of owner do you want?"

Peggy thought for a moment. A garden would be nice. So would tasty snacks.

But that wasn't what Peggy wanted most of all. At last she said, "I hope my owner loves me."

Peggy's mum gazed at her puppies tenderly, her eyes shining with affection. "That's what I want for all of you, my dears."

★ ★ ★

CLICK!

Peggy's floppy black ears perked up as she heard the key turning in the lock. It could only mean one thing – her owner was back!

"She's home!" Peggy cried, scampering around the smoky grey cat who was basking in a patch of sunlight on the floor. She batted the cat's nose with her paw. "Wake up, Misha. She's back!"

The cat opened her eyes slightly, revealing two green slivers. "Big deal," Misha hissed, swiping at Peggy with her sharp claws.

Oops, thought Peggy. Even though she had lived with the cat and her owner, Suzanne, for two months, she always forgot how grumpy Misha was when she woke up. Or any time. Unlike Peggy, the cat didn't seem to mind being left on her own for hours.

Read **The Pug Who Wanted to Be a Unicorn** to find out what happens next...

ANIMAL ARK

Where animals need you!

COLLECT ALL OF AMELIA AND SAM'S EXCITING ADVENTURES!

Kitten Rescue
Lucy Daniels

Bunny Trouble
Lucy Daniels

Fox Cub Danger
Lucy Daniels

Puppy in Peril
Lucy Daniels

The Purrfect Sleepover
Lucy Daniels

Doggy Drama
Lucy Daniels

Runaway Hamster
Lucy Daniels

Guinea Pig Superstar
Lucy Daniels

The Lonely Pony
Lucy Daniels

www.animalark.co.uk

Discover all the books in the series

Read exciting extracts

Find fun downloads

And lots more!